Shintaro Saves the Day:

A Charlie & Shintaro Adventure

Written and Illustrated By
Susan Brown-Wadleigh

ISBN: 9798838459688

DEDICATION

This is for my parents, Dean and Mary
Brown, who took us on many adventures.
The need to write this story of friendship
would not have come about without the real-
life example of Charlie the chicken and
Shintaro the duck, who taught me that
without friends life can be very dull.

To Bill, who is always in my heart, and Ben,
who is the best reflection of his father.

-

CONTENTS

Charlie

Shintaro

Prologue

Cooper's panic was not like any other. The slamming of the front doors snatched his retriever's focus from the front of the Merry-Mart to the intruders piling into the jeep. Shaken out of his daze, the dog's disbelieving eyes zeroed in on the hooded figure clambering into the passenger's side. The man twisted around to face the dog and his boy. Resting a gloved hand on the back of the seat, he pointed a gun at the young boy's innocent head. Asleep, the child woke with a start and yelled out in fear and confusion.

"Shut up," snarled the hooded figure, "or I will shoot your stupid dog!"

"Please," pleaded the boy, "don't hurt Cooper."

Stuck in the cargo area of the SUV, Cooper felt helpless. Barking, he leaped at the metal barrier that separated him from his beloved boy. It did not budge. Cooper pivoted around and began clawing at the rear window. "Tom, help, Tom, they have Ben!" The frantic dog barked for his boy's dad. As the vehicle started to speed away, the doors to the store burst open, and a man

came running out. He chased after
the jeep screaming for them to stop.
The noise from the speeding vehicle
drowned out his pleas. Cooper's
heart broke when he saw the
distraught father fall to his knees in
despair.

Chapter 1

Charlie and Shintaro

Worms squiggled through Charlie's dream. They were big, fat, juicy worms. He could see them bubbling up to the surface of the wet grass, glistening in the sunlight. Easy pickings. But suddenly, with a sharp "QUACK," Charlie's delectable dream vanished. The rooster's eyes popped open. His gaze snapped to his friend, Shintaro, who was at that moment running around in tight circles, quacking furiously, "Oh, that Lucy can make me soooooo mad!"

Clucking quietly to himself, Charlie stood up on his rubbly legs. He stretched his wings and ruffled his long, elegant tail feathers. He was not a vain rooster, but he was proud of those feathers. Charlie was especially aware of their beauty when the sun hit them just right and they danced in iridescent shades of green and purple. Charlie was a very wise and patient chicken; however, the duck's wacky morning wig-out immediately stuck in his craw. The lovely day was becoming, well, not so lovely.

On most days, Charlie and his very best friend in the whole world, the duck Shintaro, awoke to beams of morning sunlight warming their feathers. Charlie would stretch up tall as if to touch the sun, a rowdy, cock-a-doodle-do bursting forth from deep in his chest. Shintaro waddled over to his "pond" (a big, yellow, plastic tub he called his pond), and with a hop up to the edge, he would plop into the cool water for a glorious morning swim. That is how this day started.

As usual, Lucy Langdon, the birds' little girl, was prompt in bringing two bowls full of grain and cracked corn. She set the bowls down and patted the rooster and duck on the head, then dashed off to start the day. Shintaro ate, then toddled into the house to have coffee with Molly, Lucy's mom. Well, Shintaro didn't drink coffee, (might stunt his growth) but he did keep Molly company as she savored hers.

"Hello Shin!" she said as the duck head-butted his way through the swinging doggie door and waddled into the kitchen. His webbed feet slapped loudly as he crossed the old linoleum floor.

"Quack," he answered.

Molly puzzled over the crossword while Shintaro napped. They sat together in comfortable

silence until Charlie arrived. The
rooster, not quite as bold as the
duck, poked his head quietly
through the door and gently
clucked to his napping friend.
Molly gave Charlie an amused
"Good morning!" She jumped up
from the table, ready to start her
day.

As she went upstairs to
change, the two birds wended their
way out of the house, down the
stairs, and into the front yard. Most
summer days were glorious, filled
with gentle breezes, warm sun, and
soft earth. Together the birds dug
little divots in the dirt. With
feathers fluffed out, they lowered
themselves down onto their feet as
if they were on hydraulic lifts.

Wiggling their bodies back and forth in the soft dirt, they created deep imprints for their makeshift nests. The cool earth cradled them. The best buddies, comfortable at last, relaxed, and soaked up the nourishing morning sun unaware that disaster was looming.

Chapter 2

Bruno

After their sunbath, the birds wandered back to their pen. Shintaro popped into his hutch but very shortly he came popping out. He started pacing and muttering to himself. Charlie could only hear the words, "Oh, that Lucy." He tried to ignore it, but Shintaro couldn't seem to settle down.

Charlie took three deep breaths, and then said, "OK, I'll peck, what did she do?"

The now irate duck stood up on his tippy toes, stretched his neck up to the sky, threw back his wings, and wailed, "She stole my treasures! I had them all neatly tucked away, and she has taken them all!"

Charlie shook his head. "Now what did you steal?"

"I do not steal!" replied Shintaro icily. "I rescue. I recycle. I repurpose. I do not steal!"

"Call it what you like," retorted Charlie, "but Mrs. Down's

ring is missing. It is shiny. You like shiny things. And since the last several shiny things that went missing were found in your hutch, it stands to reason that Mrs. Down's ring would be there too. Ergo, you stole her ring!"

"Ergo? Really, ergo? You have got to stop watching old movies! What does that even mean, ergo?" grumbled the duck. "I still don't see why Lucy had to take it back!"

The duck lowered himself back down to normal height, waddled over to the tub, hopped in, and started to swim in fast, tight, little circles, splashing water over his oily back. "I can't believe how careless some people are. They are lucky I was the one who found their stuff!"

Shintaro's whining was interrupted by deep, threatening growls drifting down from the top of the garden wall.

"Busted again, eh, duck?" oozed the nasal voice.

The startled birds nearly dropped their tail feathers as they spun around to face the dreaded voice. A large orange paw poked out of the bush that hung over the wall. It was followed by a white-tipped ear, a pink nose, and finally the scarred body of the neighborhood bully, Bruno. He was the biggest cat either one of them had ever seen and the orneriest.

The meddlesome tabby had been a stone in the birds' gullets from the first day they had moved to the house.

"Been playing pirate again, duck?" he drawled. "Just give up. You're so bad at it."

"You steal stuff all the time!" snapped Shintaro.

"Yeah, but I never get caught. I'm too smart."

"Not smart! Sneaky and conniving maybe," quacked the duck. "Besides I'm not stealing, I'm rescuing, recycling---"

"And repurposing!" chimed in both Bruno and Charlie.

"Yup, exactly," grumbled Shintaro.

"It is not the same as stealing."

"Hey," sneered the big orange tabby, "if it waddles like a thief, and quacks like a thief..."

That was the last kernel of corn for the frustrated duck! The furious fowl rose on his toes and started to flap his wings wildly. Then, opening his beak as wide as possible, Shintaro began to hiss.

Shintaro's hiss always took Charlie by surprise. He was impressed with how fierce his friend could look. The cat, not cowed at all, jumped down from his spot on the wall and started to slink menacingly toward Shintaro.

Charlie had been careful to
stay out of the argument but now
realized, as he always did, that
Shintaro was no match for Bruno.
The duck hissed a good game, but
that was as far as it went. Before
the two foes could trade feathers
and fur, Charlie jumped in with
both feet. He spread his expansive
wings, and with a commanding
flap, he lifted his body into the air
and thrust his long, sharp talons in

front of his chest in a gesture of full-on attack. He flew at Bruno, aiming directly for his head.

Bruno, an expression of disgust on his scarred face, turned and glided back up the wall to safety, narrowly escaping the sharp claws. "Someday the chicken won't be around to save you, duck. I'll be waiting. Be afraid." He growled that deep cat growl that is all mixed up with high and low guttural, juicy, nasally, noises that sound like they are coming from deep down in the cat's belly. Then he slunk quietly off into the trees.

"O-ooh, scareeeee." Shintaro waggled his tail feathers at the retreating figure of the feline.

"You two drive me batty!" snapped Charlie as he shook his feathers back into place. "You are both all bluster and no fight. Next time you're on your own." He stomped off to his hutch, stormed up the plank, and sank into a bed of straw, grumbling to himself all the while.

"I hate everything!" quacked the duck as he padded down the path, angry and embarrassed, his black, curly tail feathers flouncing defiantly in the air.

Oh, worms! Now he's just looking for more trouble, thought Charlie as he shoved his head under his wing in hope of some peace and quiet.

Chapter 3

Cooper and the Kidnappers

Cooper barked relentlessly at the kidnappers to stop, but they continued speeding recklessly along the rural road. After what seemed like forever, the jeep pulled off onto a dirt path and bumped its way over rocky terrain. They stopped in a hidden area down a little

ravine. The kidnappers
scrambled out of the stolen
vehicle. They quickly began
throwing loose brush over it as
camouflage. While they were
distracted, Ben reached behind
his seat and loosened the
divider between the passenger
seats and the cargo area where
Cooper was anxiously pacing.
The rear door jerked open.
The taller kidnapper yanked
Ben out of the car. The other
shoved a brown cloth bag over
the frightened boy's head. The
two dragged him to a pickup
truck hidden behind some
boulders. A third person
seated behind the steering
wheel revved the engine as the
kidnappers pushed young Ben

into the back seat.

The terrified dog began to howl. Then with all the strength, he could muster, Cooper threw his trembling body against the divider. That did it! The barrier gave way and Cooper flew out of the Jeep. He ran up the hill just in time to see the green truck pull away. The dog did not hesitate. He bounded onto the road and ran as fast as he could to catch the fleeing vehicle. As the truck picked up speed Cooper could see it slipping farther away from him.

Just when he thought all hope was lost, the driver slammed on the brakes to avoid hitting a cattle truck entering the intersection. Cooper gathered his strength for a final sprint. He caught up to the truck just in time to jump into the back. With all the mooing coming from the cattle and the radio blaring from the pickup's cabin, no one heard the dog as he thunked, exhausted, into the empty truck bed.

The Ford pick-up with its four stressed-out humans and one frantic canine drove for a long time, climbing higher and higher into the mountains. Eventually, they stopped to open a gate. Then they bounced along a well-hidden dirt driveway that meandered through a thick copse of trees. The truck came to an abrupt halt in front of a cluster of buildings tucked in a small clearing in the woods.

The three captors tumbled out

of the car. Two headed to a cabin, and one reached into the backseat dragging Ben out by the arm. As they turned towards the building, Cooper jumped out of the back of the truck, landing on the head of the kidnapper. Ben broke loose and ran toward the cover of the dense woods as his captor tried to fight off Cooper's fierce attack.

Alerted by the shouts, the other two kidnappers rushed out of the cabin to aid their friend. One perpetrator took off after Ben. The other looked around for some way to stop the ferocious dog. Grabbing a thick branch from the ground the would-be captor began swinging at Cooper, but he couldn't get a good solid hit without striking the canine's victim. Finally, the combatants broke away long enough for the stick-wielding villain to land one sound blow upon the heroic beast. This stopped Cooper for a minute, but before he could recover, the kidnappers were hitting him. He soon felt the world going dark. The last thing the poor dog remembered was being dragged into the woods. Then all went black.

Chapter 4

Trouble

Shintaro slapped his big feet heavily in the dirt as he sulked down the path away from Charlie. He hopped up the ancient wooden stairs to the porch and peered through the screen door at the cozy kitchen. He saw that Lucy was taking inventory of his purloined trinkets.

"Not quite as impressive as usual," muttered Lucy to her mother.

Harumph, thought Shintaro, *I'd like to see her do better!*

"The gold orby thingy from Mrs. Roger's lawn, the doohickey from Mr. B's toolbox, and the bonnet off of Mrs. Tyler's goofy, plastic goose," Lucy listed as she continued to unpack the treasures. When she moved the tiny, purple, polka-dotted bonnet, something heavy and metallic fell out of its folds. "Oh, oh, it's Mrs. Down's ring."

Her mother peered over her shoulders at the dirt-covered jewel. "Oh dear, you'd better return those things right away. I'll make pies to take over later as a way of apology."

"Apology indeed!" sputtered the duck. "They owe me one and a thank you too!" He turned abruptly around and there in front of him was a sight for revengeful eyes: long, bare legs ending at a set of gleaming bedazzled toenails. Under the feet were tall heels that came to the sharpest, deadliest point the duck had ever seen. The body, perched dangerously on these stilts, bobbled and wobbled toward him.

Shintaro did not recognize the unsteady human, so he did what any self-respecting guard duck would do: he lowered his body down close to his feet to lock in his center of gravity. Next, he stretched his neck straight out in front of him for balance. With all systems go, his feet started flapping fast and furious, whirling his little body toward the unsuspecting stranger.

The woman wearing the wobbly shoes was so wrapped up in her thoughts that she did not notice the feathered missile hurtling toward her until she felt the first hot, pinch on the tender skin of her ankle. She squawked in alarm and began flailing her large, pink, patent leather purse as the attack continued, sharp and furious, against her unprotected feet and legs. Finally, she threw her hands in the air and, screaming, flew down the path to the garden gate.

She was running, jumping, and
kicking all at the same time, her
arms waving in a windmill motion
as the feisty fowl nipped at her
fleeing feet. The duck kept up the
unrelenting attack until he ran
headfirst into the fence. The
trespasser had untangled herself
enough to run through the open
gate and shut it quickly behind her.

"Whoops, a new victim. I
guess she didn't believe the
'Beware of Duck' sign," muttered
Lucy as she and her mother ran
down the steps to the front gate.

"Lucy, stop that right now and
get your duck," scolded her mother.

Lucy scooped up her
squirming pet. She stroked his

ruffled feathers and told him loudly what a good and brave duck he was. Shintaro, panting hard from his ferocious pursuit, glared at the stranger from Lucy's protective arms.

"I am so sorry," gushed Molly to the stranger.

"Madam, that animal is a menace! It should be boiled alive!" shrieked the hysterical woman as she checked her body for damage.

Molly stopped mid-apology. Her jaw set and her voice cold, she said, "If you had read the sign posted at the gate, you would have been warned. There is a doorbell on the fence so that we can escort welcomed visitors to our door.

Now, is there something I can do for you?"

The woman sputtered for a second or two, then replied, "Do you own that store?" she pointed to the building a few yards from the house.

"Yes," Molly replied.

"Well, I need to get some things," snapped the woman.

Molly stated firmly that it did not open for another half hour and that her son would unlock the doors at that time. The woman insisted that she must get in now, that she needed supplies for a camping trip and could not wait. Molly stood her ground and repeated the store hours.

The woman, furious at this refusal, flounced away shouting over her shoulder, "I'd keep an eye on that duck if I were you. I am sure it would make a delicious pâté!"

As the woman trotted toward her car, Molly turned abruptly on her heels. She patted the head of the panting bird. "Good work, Shin," she said under her breath. Then she stalked angrily up the front steps to the house and slammed the screen door behind her.

Chapter 5

Lucy's Story

Lucy carried Shintaro over to the ancient walnut tree. Still cradling her pet in her arms, she sat down with her back against the rough trunk. Gently, Lucy scratched her duck's head. The little bird bent forward so that she would be sure to get the exact spot. He closed his eyes, calm for the first time that day.

"Shin, I'm sure that lady deserved to have her ankles pinched. I know that you are trying to live up to your namesake, Shintaro, the Samuri, but you have to stop doing that stuff." Shintaro blinked his eyes at her. "Mom doesn't want to give you away, Shin. You are very special to all of us. Dad gave you to me because you reminded him of me. Dad always said," here the girl lowered her voice in imitation of her father, "He was the only yellow and black duckling in the pond, and he was so plucky and curious that he reminded me of you, Lucy."

She lowered her head against the duck's. Shintaro felt a teardrop.

He knew how much she missed her father. They all did: he, Charlie, Elliot, and Molly. Shintaro had been a gift to Lucy when he was just a small duckling, and Charlie had come to them soon after, as a rescue. They had all lived together happily on a big farm until Henry had slipped in the barn while tending to a frightened cow.

Three years had passed since Henry's death. They had to sell the farm after the first year, for it was too much for Molly to handle with the two children, Elliot and Lucy. She bought a general store in a small town. It catered to the locals and the summer campers. It was a feed, grocery, and hardware store, plus the post office all in one.

Their store was one of the few places to buy supplies for several miles, so it kept busy. Elliot was very involved in the running of it. He had been a great source of strength during the last three terrible years. Many times, Shintaro had heard Molly say she didn't know what she would have done without him.

Although she put up a good front, Charlie and Shintaro were especially worried about Lucy. She had changed. The once happy, curious, energetic little girl had turned inward. She did as she was told, completed her chores, and did her homework. But the twinkle in her eye was gone. Charlie and Shintaro were happy that she still talked to them, and they knew she loved them more than anything, but they were her only friends.

Chapter 6

Disgruntled

Lucy wearily carried the duck back to his pen. "Try to behave Shintaro," she admonished. "No more "rescuing" things or attacking people's feet. The neighbors are getting pretty annoyed."

The unrepenting duck waddled over to his tub, hopped in,

and started dunking his head under the cool water.

Lucy sighed in exasperation. "You need to keep a better eye on him, Charlie," she said. "He listens to you." Then she turned and trudged down the path toward the store, prepared to take an earful from her mom.

Charlie tipped his head reproachfully, but before he even opened his beak, Shintaro said, "I don't want to hear it!"

Charlie said, "Fine!" And that was it. They each sat in their respective corners of the pen and sulked, refusing to speak to each other for the rest of the morning.

Chapter 7

The Stranger

Shintaro was a very grumpy duck. Nothing was right: the water in his tub was too cold or too hot; the grain mixture needed more corn or had too much corn, and the hay in his bedding was too pokey. He wiggled and paced. He sighed and hissed. He stared at the boring walls of the little hutch. He wanted out. Shintaro the duck needed an adventure.

Charlie recognized all the symptoms; the pacing, the sighing, the shorter naps, the trips to and from the fence, the long walks up and down the fence, the pacing, the sighing…. Charlie did everything he could to distract his friend. He tried to hide Shintaro's toys so that he would have to hunt for them. He floated sticks in the tub, which usually made Shintaro mad and kept him occupied for a while trying to get them out (he liked a very clean tub). Charlie even welcomed Bruno when he came to harass them. Shintaro didn't react to the quarrelsome feline. Bruno slunk away dejected, muttering that he'd get that "dumb duck" next time. Finally, around sunset, Charlie gave up, fluttered to his favorite branch in his favorite tree, tucked his head under the warm feathers of his wing, and fell asleep.

Shintaro, on the other hand, sat there and festered. He tried to cuddle under his wing, but the little down feathers underneath poked and needled him until he could no longer stand it. He carefully rose onto his webbed feet and quietly padded out of the pen to the path below. He zipped through the secret hole in the fence behind the lilac bush. He popped out the other side and looked both ways. Anywhere would do. He took one step, then erupted into a wobbly duck run. He was free!

The little duck felt much better. No one to fuss at him or nag. The moon was shining full and bright. He gleefully hopped through puddles leftover from the previous night's rain. He chased bunny rabbits, avoided owls, and finally felt himself again.

Soon Shintaro wandered into the woods. He trundled through some very thick undergrowth and followed the moonlight to a clearing. He was just about to explore deeper when his foot landed on something soft and furry. He jumped back and turned to run, but then he heard a low moan. He could not help himself; he had to investigate.

He had stepped on a long, low lump that was connected to a bigger fuzzy lump. There was no movement and no more sounds from it, so he gently nudged the thing with his hard, stubby beak. Gleaming fangs filled his vision, and Shintaro jumped back, shouting, "Wait! No! I want to help you." The jaws were already closing over his head, but the beast stopped just in time. Hot breath washed over Shintaro, and a trickle of drool plopped onto his head.

"Please! I can help you!" repeated the terrified bird, his long neck squished down into his body and his eyes closed tight. The jaws pulled away, and the beast slumped back down to the ground.

"How can you help me, you small, insignificant snack?" it growled. As the stranger sat, the moonlight reflected off its black fur and glinted on something shiny and red: blood. Shintaro stared at the injured dog.

In Shintaro's experience, cats were merely an annoyance, but dogs could mean real trouble. Shintaro really, really wanted to run away, but the more he looked at the dog, the more he realized that this animal was badly hurt. He saw blood oozing from one of its ears and cuts on its paws.

"I may be insignificant, but I live near here, and I have a little girl who could probably help you," answered the duck.

The confused canine looked over his shoulder and whispered in desperation, "I can't leave my little boy. He is in trouble and needs me. They are holding him captive in that house in the woods."

Ducks weren't made for this sort of thing, so he sat and pondered what the dog had said for a minute. "Well," replied Shintaro, "I'm not very smart, but even I can see that you can't be of any help to your boy with all that yuck sliding down your head. So, let's go get you fixed up first and then figure out what to do. My friend Charlie is smart. I bet he can help us. Are you strong enough to follow me back to my family?"

The injured dog said that he would try, and the two of them slowly headed for the Langdon homestead.

Chapter 8

Getting Help

Shintaro had not kept track of how far away he was from home. When he was just having fun, it hadn't mattered, but now, with a wounded dog following slowly behind him, he felt like home was miles and miles away. The time dragged on. Every puddle seemed deeper and gooier, every brush

thicker and pokier, and every tree
bigger and scarier. By the time they
made it back to the fence in front of
the Langdon house, the exhausted
dog was barely able to walk. He
was too weak to climb the fence.
Shintaro left him there and ran to
the pen to wake Charlie.

Now, waking Charlie was
never an easy or wise thing to do.
Although chickens like to rise
early, they never like to be woken
before the sun comes up. When
Charlie stopped squawking long
enough for Shintaro to get a word
in edgewise, the now alert chicken
was quick to jump down from his
tree and hurry to the front gate.

Charlie was a very smart bird
and had observed the humans

opening this very gate, hundreds of times. He flew up to the top of the gate post then jumped onto the little lever until it popped up, releasing the catch. The gate swung open. Shintaro urged the wounded dog through it and guided him carefully toward their pen. They brought him to their trough of water and watched as he drank deeply from it. Barely strong enough to finish lapping up the water, the careworn canine dropped to the ground.

"My name is Cooper," the exhausted dog whispered, "I need help…my boy." then he fell into a restless sleep.

While they watched over the dog, Shintaro filled Charlie in on his exciting adventure.

"Wow, he does need help!" exclaimed the chicken. "First things first though, he needs medical attention, toot sweet!" (This was one of Charlie's favorite old human sayings. He had learned it from Lucy's grandmother).

Shintaro had been out so long that daylight was peeking over the horizon. Charlie clucked, "Lucy will be waking up soon. We need her out here as quickly as possible. I'll get her."

The chicken raced across the yard and fluttered up to Lucy's windowsill on the first floor. He held onto the old wood frame with his long talons and began pecking at the windowpane. When he got no response, he began tapping

harder. Soon Lucy began to stir.
She looked around in a sleepy haze,
then spotted the chicken on her
windowsill. She got up slowly and
pushed open the window.

Charlie wasted no time but
began fluttering toward the bird
pen. When Lucy didn't follow, he
hurried back to her, then darted
toward the pen again.

Realizing that something must
be wrong, Lucy threw on her
sneakers and a bathrobe. She ran
outside to where the chicken was
anxiously waiting for her.

The sun broke over the
horizon just as Lucy got to the
bird's pen, so she could easily see
the dog next to Shintaro's tub. She

stopped. Her dad had taught her to always approach a sleeping or possibly wounded animal with extreme caution.

"Hello," whispered the girl, "my name is Lucy. Are you all right?" She took a few small steps toward the dog. Charlie and Shintaro followed closely behind her quacking and clucking encouragement. When she was finally just a few feet away she repeated, "Are you all right? I am here to help you."

The dog opened his eyes and very weakly wagged his tail. Lucy left to bring him more water. She set the replenished bowl in front of the wounded animal then knelt beside him. As she gently patted his soft black fur the worried child noticed the dried blood on his ear, head, and paws.

"I need to get help," She told the birds. Then she ran toward the house, yelling, "Mom, Elliot, you had better come quick."

In just a few minutes, Molly and Elliot, both dressed in bathrobes and slippers, were standing over the injured dog in the bird's pen, assessing the situation.

"I'm afraid to move him in case something is broken," said Molly. "Elliot, call Dr. Mary. See if she can make a house call." Within half an hour, the veterinarian was kneeling beside the injured dog.

"He has a few cuts and

bruises; he needs to rest for a while." She cleaned up his wounds and gave him an injection of antibiotics and a sedative to help him sleep.

They moved the patient onto a blanket. Then the four humans carried the unconscious dog into the kitchen.

"I wonder how he got here and what happened to him? You said there was no collar, and I can't find any sign of an identification chip in his neck." said Dr. Mary, "Also, why are the chicken and duck so calm around him?"

"I doubt we will ever know," said Molly. She poured coffee for herself and Mary. The two women

sat at the kitchen table quietly
watching as Lucy, now settled on
the blanket next to the big dog,
stroked him gently as he slept.

Chapter 9

Cooper's Story

Late that afternoon, Big Dog (the temporary name Lucy and Elliot had given Cooper) woke up, found the doggie door, and stumbled his way back to Charlie and Shintaro, who were napping in their pen.

"You've got to help me," he whined, shuffling from foot to foot.

Charlie stood, eyeing the dog warily. "Help with what?"

"There's no time, please," Cooper said as he paced back and forth in front of the two bewildered birds.

"Take a deep breath. Let's all calmly review the situation," suggested Charlie, but Shintaro hopped up.

"What do you need help with exactly?"

"I will tell you the whole story, but I need you to take me back to where you found me. That is close to where my boy is. We have to get back there now!" he urged. "Lead the way, duck!"

Charlie hesitated, but Shintaro nodded enthusiastically. "Let's go!"

Cooper and Charlie fell in behind Shintaro as the plucky duck led them all back to the woods. While the three wended their way through the prickly underbrush Cooper began to tell his tale.

"My name is Cooper," he started. "My boy, Ben, was stolen by some bad people." Charlie and Shintaro listened in horror as the distraught dog described the canine versus human battle and the final blow that sent him into blackness.

"And that's the end of it," concluded the dog.

"It is not," said Shintaro,

poking Cooper in the stomach with his stubby beak. "Don't forget the part where you almost ate me!"

Chapter 10

Finding Ben

Shintaro led them to the clump of trees where he had first discovered Cooper. Then the big black retriever's instincts kicked in. He sniffed around, trying to catch the scent of the pickup truck or Ben. He ran through the woods, nose to the ground. Charlie and Shintaro followed closely behind.

It was just about dusk when they arrived at the cabin. The truck was not there, but smoke was coming out of the chimney and lights glowed from inside. Shintaro sneaked up to the front door to see if it was open. The screen door was shut, but the latch looked simple if they could get high enough to push on it. Cooper peeked into the main window of the cabin. He saw a man sleeping on a couch. In front of him, a small television perched precariously on a rickety folding table. Charlie, meanwhile, scampered around to the back of the building. He climbed atop some garbage cans, then fluttered up to a high window. There was Ben! He was handcuffed to an old brass bed. The door leading into the room was

closed. The only other way in was
an old slider window that looked as
if it had not been opened in years.
While Charlie was watching, Ben
wiggled a piece of the bed frame
until it lifted away from the base.
He slid the handcuffs through the
gap and stood.

Charlie jumped down from the
window. He met up with his friends
to tell them the good news. As they
put their furry and feathered heads
together to come up with a plan,
they heard a twig snap!

The three rescuers wheeled
around and found themselves face
to face with Lucy.

She was dirty and scratched
up from scrambling through the

brush. Her ball cap was twisted sideways. She had her hands on her hips, and a scowl on her face. "You are a long way from home. What are you three up to?" Charlie clucked and started toward the back of the cabin. His two companions and Lucy crouched low and followed quietly. Charlie fluttered onto the garbage cans once again and back up to the windowsill. Lucy followed, trying not to make noise.

Lucy was shocked to see a boy in the dreary little room. She slid off the can and followed Cooper to the front of the cabin, and together they peeked through the window at the man. He was talking on his phone.

"We need to move the kid tonight. Get here around ten and we can take him up in the mountains," said the kidnapper. "Once you are sure the ransom's safe, we can tell 'dad' where to find his boy. Is everything all set? … Good. I'll see you then." He walked into the tiny kitchen where he dumped a can of soup into a bowl, popped it in the microwave, and pushed the start button. Returning to the couch the man snatched up a ski mask from the floor, pulled it on, and strode toward the door of Ben's cell. Upon hearing the keys jangle the boy quickly sat down on the bed. He had just enough time to put the cuffs back in place and slip the bedpost together. The jailer drew back the bolt and shoved the door open. "Just checking to see if you are awake," he said to the boy. This time when he spoke, the man's voice was raspy, and he had a southern drawl. *He didn't talk like that earlier,* Lucy thought, *maybe that's a good sign. Maybe, if he is going to all the trouble of disguising his voice, they don't intend to harm that boy.*

"I'm bringing you some soup, so sit up," the jailer commanded. He grabbed the bowl from the microwave and set the meager meal on the floor by the old bed. He then bolted the door shut again, leaving the boy alone in the darkening room.

Chapter 11

The Rescue

Lucy headed stealthily back toward the woods with the menagerie in tow. When they reached a clearing, the girl, the dog, and the chicken circled together to try to come up with a plan. "Where's Shintaro?" asked Lucy. As she looked around, she spied a very distracted duck. The silly bird was splashing in a mud puddle

while he chased the shiny reflection
of the moon as it danced in the
murky water.

"We have to let that boy know
we're here," said Lucy. "I need
something to write with." She
checked her pockets, but they were
empty. Just then Shintaro began
shaking his whole body to rid it of
the gooey mud. Big globules of the
slippery, brown liquid flew
everywhere landing on the group as
they watched in disgust. Then Lucy
began to laugh. "Shin, you are
brilliant!" She took off her Tony
Stewart baseball cap and started to
scoop up mud with it.

All four rescuers scrambled
back to the side of the cabin.
Cooper and Shintaro snuck around

the front to keep watch on the main entrance while Charlie and Lucy scurried toward the back. Once again, Lucy used the handy garbage cans to climb up to the window. *I'm getting very good at this,* she thought as she tapped gingerly on the grubby windowpane. Ben, busy trying to get the bed apart, jumped and looked nervously around for the noise. When he saw the wild, dirty little face up high in the window, he almost shrieked in terror.

Lucy held her finger to her lips, then began writing on the window with the brown goo from her hat. It wasn't easy. She had to write backward so he could read it. Finally, she was able to get the message across: "Here to help. U need out now. Window?"

Ben glanced at the door, raised his right index finger, and turned back to the bedpost. In a few seconds, he had it apart enough to slide his handcuffs up and out. Quickly and quietly the boy moved to the cobwebbed and dust-encrusted window. It was too high up for him to reach the latch. He glanced around the room looking for something he could stand on. The bed was too big to move, but there were three large cardboard boxes in the corner. They were full of papers and magazines and seemed sturdy enough. They were heavy, so he first dragged all three under the window, then unpacked

one partway to make it lighter.
Once it was in place, he filled it
back up and managed to get the
smallest box on top. It wasn't
completely stable, but it was tall
enough. Ben eagerly reached for
the window. He unlatched it, but
even with Lucy helping to push he
couldn't slide the old pane
sideways to get it open. Years of
dried paint had made the window
impossible to budge. Ben crept
down the boxes and began
searching for something he could
use to chip away the paint.

Meanwhile, Cooper and
Shintaro had eyes on the captor in
the front room. The man seemed to
be asleep, but suddenly he sat up
and reached for his shoes and

mask. Cooper ran silently to Lucy and spun in circles below, trying to warn her. Lucy tapped urgently on the window and pointed toward the door. Ben barely had time to slip back into his handcuffs before the man came into the room. He held his breath, but the man didn't seem to notice the boxes piled under the window. Instead, the clueless captor focused on the still-full bowl of soup on the floor.

"What's the matter? Don't you like bean soup? Come on, I'm going to take you to the outhouse." He unlocked the boy's handcuffs and led him through the cabin and out the front door to a smelly privy a short distance away.

Cooper and Shintaro had

already hurried back to their post at the front of the cabin. The screen door was slightly ajar, and Shintaro wiggled through.

"Get out of there," growled Cooper, but the curious duck began cheerfully poking his beak into anything that looked interesting. Cooper heard the boy and his captor coming back. "Get out now," he growled, but there was no time. The big dog slipped off the side of the porch and around the corner of the cabin. By the time Shintaro realized what was happening, it was too late. The man's feet were clomping up the porch steps. Shintaro flapped his wings in alarm, then darted to the nearest hiding place. He shimmied under the dusty yellow sofa and tried to breathe a sigh of relief, but the space was too tight.

"You'd better eat your soup," the man grumbled. He attached Ben to the bed again. "Also try to get some sleep. It's going to be a long night, and you'll be needing your strength." With that, he left the boy alone and bolted the door.

As soon as he heard the TV blaring, Ben wasted no time in slipping his cuffs off the bedpost. He grabbed the soup spoon and climbed back up to the window. He began scraping at the paint with the spoon handle. It was tedious work, but he kept at it. Charlie 'brukked' encouragingly from outside.

Ben dug at the layers of dried paint with all his might. He was sweating, his breathing ragged and his fingers bruised and bloodied. He was nervous that now it was dark the other kidnappers would be back soon. Lucy kept her face close to the window so Ben would know she was still there. "Hurry, kid!" she whispered, "Hurry!"

Charlie thought of Saturday morning cartoons as he watched the boy's hands digging with lighting speed, paint chips flying all around his curly head. With one final crack and groan the old window started to move. The two children pushed hard to get it open. Just as Ben hoisted himself up through the window, the kidnapper came bursting through the door. The furious captor was in time to see the soles of Ben's tennis shoes as they kicked over the boxes and slipped away through the gapping portal into the night.

With a scream of anger and frustration the man turned and ran through the house to the front door.

"Shintaro!" barked Cooper from the front window, "You've got to stop him!"

The tenacious little duck shimmied out from under the sofa, pulled himself up to his full height, and attacked. With flapping wings, enraged quacks, and hisses, he lunged at the fleeing figure, his beak pinching away at the man's legs and hands. With arms flailing all around him the man tried to fight off the attacking duck as he stumbled onto the porch.

At that moment, the pickup

truck came screeching to a stop at the cabin door. The other kidnappers tumbled out. One ran toward his friend and the attacking duck. The one in the driver's seat reached across the cab to the glove compartment. As the co-captor fumbled with the latch, Cooper jumped through the open door. With his nose curled into a snarl, and his hair standing on end, he looked like a bear. The terrified driver jumped out of the truck and sprinted toward the cabin with Cooper close behind.

Charlie joined the fray by flying, talons first, at the villain heading for Shintaro. He clung to the front of the kidnapper's coveralls. With his short but sharp beak, he pecked unmercifully at the ski mask. His impressively long wings flapped, making it difficult for the culprit to see.

Shintaro's assailant was finally able to connect his right fist with the brave duck's fragile body. The lucky punch sent the stunned bird flying into the side of the truck where his bruised little body slid down the door and seemed to melt into a pile of gasping feathers. Free of the duck, the kidnapper yanked the attacking chicken off his friend and threw the screeching bird against a nearby tree. When the two battered thieves saw the very large, angry dog leaping at them, they turned and ran. They stumbled their way to the back room where Ben

had been held captive. The terrified
kidnappers lunged through the
door. It was comical to see the
three pivot in unison, slam the door
shut, and throw their heaving
bodies against it to keep away from
the ferocious canine. However,
Cooper trotted calmly to the door,
and with his big, black, shiny nose
shoved the bolt into place, locking
the kidnappers in. He knew it was
only temporary, but it might buy
the fleeing children some time. The
dog rushed back outside to see if
his new friends were all right.
Shintaro was still leaning against
the truck gasping for air. The poor
battered duck had had the wind
knocked out of him when he hit the
side of the pickup, but otherwise,
he was fine.

Charlie, on the other hand, was badly hurt. The courageous bird was lying on the ground beneath the tree, with his wing hanging limply at his side. "I think they broke my wing," he said calmly.

Cooper looked at the mess of feathers, "Yes, I think you're right," he replied. "Let's get you back to your house and see about getting us all some help. Ben and Lucy should have made it home by now." The gentle dog lay down on his side next to the wounded bird. "Hop on board," he urged. Charlie struggled to his feet. Shintaro came up behind him and nudged his friend onto the big dog's back. "Try to hang on as best you can," cautioned Cooper. Charlie dug his claws into the thick fur. "Ow, not that hard!"

Suddenly there was a loud hissing, a bloodcurdling scream, and then a huge clatter and crashing from the back of the cabin. When Shintaro, Cooper, and Charlie rounded the corner of the house, they saw a bloodied arm slip back down through the small window into Ben's former prison. A big yellow tabby cat was sitting calmly amongst the toppled garbage cans.

"Well," he purred as he nonchalantly cleaned his face with his big paw, "I didn't see why you three should have all the fun. Besides, it looked like you were about to make a mess of this too.

Just like always."

Both Charlie and Shintaro said, 'Oh worms!" at the same time.

"Who is that?" asked Cooper.

"That thing is Bruno, the neighborhood bully," said Shintaro.

"This neighborhood bully just saved your big feathery behinds," jeered Bruno.

"Well, I for one thank you," said Cooper. "Now we have to see where our humans are." He turned and headed determinedly back through the woods, careful of the wounded chicken riding on his back.

Shintaro said, "Go ahead. I'll

catch up in a minute." Turning on his big, webbed feet, the duck trotted back toward the abandoned pickup truck.

Chapter 12

Home at Last

Lucy and Elliot sat on the edge of the porch wrapped in blankets, watching the lane for their heroes. They had wanted to run back to see if the animals needed help, but Molly would not allow the children out of her sight. When they saw the bedraggled heroes in the light of a streetlamp, Lucy and

Elliot ran down the porch steps and out to the street to meet them.

Bruno snarled, "Well, this is where I get off. I can see it's gonna get way too sappy for me. You owe me one." With that, the big, orange tabby cat bounded up the nearest tree and hid in the leaves.

Lucy got to the group first, picked up Shintaro, who had finally caught up with his slow-moving friends, and hugged him. Then she saw Charlie. She carefully placed Shintaro in Elliot's arms and knelt next to Cooper. She patted his head and thanked him for taking care of her friends. When she looked at Charlie's wing, she began to cry. She took off the blanket from her shoulders and carefully wrapped it around the wounded bird. She held him close to her chest as the ragged group walked slowly up to the house.

When Molly heard the children's cries she rushed out on to the front porch . With one look at Lucy's tear-streaked face she immediately ran back inside to call the vet. Elliot gently set Shintaro on the porch and took Cooper into the kitchen to find Ben.

The boy, seated in a rocking chair, was wrapped tightly in a colorful afghan. Sheriff Dean sat talking with him about his horrible ordeal. When Ben saw Cooper, he flew out of the rocker and threw his arms around the dirty, tired, but happy dog. The sheriff stood, gathered up his hat, and with a grim expression, said, "I'm going to head to the cabin. See what my men have found out. I'll leave Deputy Swinney posted out front. When the FBI arrives, I know they'll want to talk to you, Ben." The sheriff looked into the boy's anxious eyes. "We have put roadblocks up. We'll catch them, young man. Don't you worry." He patted Ben's shoulder, set his white Stetson squarely on his gray head, and disappeared out the kitchen door.

Dr. Mary told Molly she would meet them at her surgery right away. Elliot drove their dad's old truck up to the gate, jumped out, and held the door open for his sister and her patient. Lucy climbed into the front seat with Charlie. Ben ran out of the house to the truck. Stretching his hand through the window the grateful boy patted the chicken's head.

"Thanks for rescuing me," Ben said. Then he looked at Lucy. She had tears running down her face.

"His name is Charlie," she sobbed.

"He'll be all right, Lucy. Thank you. I owe everything to you and your friends."

Elliot turned the ignition key. After a couple of coughs and sputters, the old truck took off, bouncing down the road to the vet clinic. Shintaro and Cooper stood on the porch and stared after the ancient pickup with its precious cargo until they could no longer see the taillights. The dog and the bird settled down together on the blanket left for them. They waited in silence for Charlie to return.

Chapter 13

Reunion

Ben rested in the big recliner in the Langdon's cozy living room. The exhausted child tried very hard to stay awake until his dad got there, but soon his eyes began to close.

Molly busied herself making coffee, and baking goodies. FBI agents had been by earlier, spoken for a few minutes with Ben, and headed up to the cabin site where Sheriff Dean was. More and more official cars were coming into the small town. This was the most activity the town had seen since the terrible flooding of 1964. Elliot called to say that Dr. Mary was setting Charlie's wing. The vet thought the chicken would be all right in a few weeks. Elliot reported that Charlie was being a very cooperative patient. Cooper finally went into the living room and settled down next to his boy. Shintaro sat alone on the porch and watched the road.

It seemed like hours and hours, but eventually, Shintaro's vigil ended when the truck pulled up the drive. Shintaro followed as Lucy carried Charlie into the house, his wing set and wrapped in bandages. Elliot fixed up a box with hay for a makeshift nest. The family wanted to keep an eye on Charlie and knew that Shintaro would not leave his side. Elliot went up to bed, but Lucy asked if she could sleep in the living room with Ben. After a few minutes, Lucy was in pajamas snuggled down in her sleeping bag next to the birds' box and Ben's chair. The living room was getting crowded.

At about three in the morning, after Molly had taken the last tray of cookies from the oven, she heard a car door slam shut. She went expectantly out onto the front porch. A man sprinted through the gate and ran up the path to the house. He took the porch steps in a single bound.

"I'm Tom Lawrence; where is my son?" he demanded.

"He's asleep in the living room," said Molly. She opened the door for the relieved father who was next to his son in three long strides. He bent down and scooped the sleeping child up in his arms, tears streaming down his face. Ben woke, saw he was in his father's familiar, reassuring embrace, and began to cry as he wrapped his arms around his dad's neck.

"I love you dad," he sobbed. Tom slumped down into the big

chair with his precious child still held tightly in his arms. They cried together until Ben began to snore.

After a while Molly heard Tom whisper, "My arm is asleep, but I'm afraid to move. He looks like he did when he was a baby."

Molly smiled and suggested, "Why don't you put him on the sofa and come into the kitchen for a cup of coffee. I can fill you in on what's happened. Oh, be careful of the sleeping girl, dozing dog, and box of birds." After Tom had moved his son, he kissed the child's head and joined Molly in the kitchen.

Molly and Tom were still there drinking coffee, eating

cookies, and talking, when Sheriff Dean and FBI Agent Burr arrived. The two law officers reported that the cabin was secured. They had found the truck a few miles away from the crime scene. It was cleaned out. A forensic team had been able to find partial tread marks from a different vehicle close by. They made a plaster cast of the tire prints in hopes of discovering the make and model of the getaway car. There were roadblocks set up everywhere, but so far, no leads. Tom was told he could take Ben home anytime. The FBI would contact them when they had more information. Then all the officials left.

"It looks like the kids will be

asleep for a while. Stretch out on the recliner so you can be near Ben and get a nap at least," suggested Molly. Tom thanked her and settled down to rest.

Chapter 14

Saying Goodbye

Tom woke the next morning to sunlight streaming in the window and his child curled up on his lap. He thought that he had never had a happier awakening. The little boy, with soft curls and big brown eyes, looked into his dad's loving face.

"Hi, Dad. I'm so glad you're

here. Is Mom here too?"

"She's on her way, Ben. She'll meet us at home. She couldn't get an earlier flight out, but she's on the plane now."

Lucy bounded into the sunny room. "Good morning Mr. Lawrence."

Ben jumped up to stand by her. "Dad, this is my rescuer, Lucy."

Tom Lawrence stood up and walked to the little girl. He knelt in front of her, took hold of her hands, and said, "Lucy, I owe everything to you. Thank you just isn't enough. I will be forever beholden to you and your funny feathered friends."

"Don't forget Cooper," added Lucy with a proud smile. "He showed us where Ben was." Tom laughed and enfolded both children into his big bear-like arms. He held on to them for what seemed like ages. Finally, they all broke apart and smiled shyly at each other.

"Mom's got pancakes and bacon cooking for anyone who wants some," reported Lucy.

"I'm in," said Tom.

After breakfast, Lucy and Ben checked on the birds in their pen. Charlie was in an old dog kennel so he wouldn't move about too much while his wing healed. He looked comfortable. Shintaro stayed close by.

At one o'clock Tom and Ben, with Cooper in tow, climbed into Tom's black BMW in preparation for the three-hour drive back to their home. Before they left, Ben asked Lucy if he could email her. She said she would like that. Then after handshakes and hugs all around, they were gone. Life went on.

Chapter 15

End of Summer

The next day, Lucy received an email from Ben telling her that he had arrived home safely. A few days later, he told her that his mom had gotten back from her photography assignment, and he would be staying at her house for a while. He began emailing Lucy, sometimes in the middle of the night when he woke up from nightmares, but most of the time, they exchanged emails about their daily lives. Lucy told him about helping at the store and Shintaro's latest escapade. Ben wrote about Cooper, and the Ford Mustang he and his dad were repairing. They even talked about more serious things like Ben's parents' divorce and Lucy's father's death. They didn't know it, but Tom and Molly were talking almost as much.

The summer went on. There had been no further news of the kidnappers. Lucy was soon able to take off Charlie's bandages. It was reported that the wing was almost good as new. Cooper did not have any lasting effects from the beating he had taken. Lucy and Elliot built a "tree" for Charlie to roost in while he recovered by nailing scraps of wood together. It looked kind of silly, but it was sturdy and short enough for Charlie to climb on without the risk of falling. Molly affectionately called it the Charlie Brown Christmas tree. After about a month, Charlie was feeling more like himself again. Bruno continued to stop by to tease the birds, but his gruffness didn't seem so mean anymore.

Near the end of the summer, Molly invited Ben and Tom for a visit. Neither Molly nor Tom were sure what Ben's reaction would be to returning to the scene of his kidnapping, but Ben, when asked,

said he thought he would be fine.
He wanted to see Lucy again. He
knew that she was the only one
who really understood how he felt.
More importantly, they had become
very good friends.

Chapter 16

Shintaro Shares a Secret

Ben's visit was still a few days away when Charlie was woken from a nap by the persistent sound of Shintaro digging. Quietly he stood and eased closer to where Shintaro was diligently working. When he finally said, "Whatcha doin'?" he had to jump back to avoid the duck's surprised flapping.

"What, what, there's nothing here. I've got nothing here. Go away, shoo!"

"Wow," retorted Charlie as he stood at a safe distance from the manic bird. "Shoo huh? For someone who is not hiding anything, methinks thou doth protest too much," he scoffed, quoting something that Molly often said to the kids.

"Nope! There is nothing to see here. So just be on your way."

"Now Shintaro, you really think after all these years I don't know when you are hiding something?" asked Charlie. "You have been way too content to stay within the confines of the fence these past few weeks. You must have something special hidden in there. Let's see it."

Shintaro looked dubiously at his friend then said, "OK." He scurried into the back of his hutch, moved some hay aside, and then began to push the soft earth around. After a few minutes of careful digging, he emerged triumphantly. Dangling from his dirt-encrusted beak was a long chain with something round hanging down. After being buried in the ground for several weeks, Shintaro's treasure did not look too impressive.

"Wow, that is quite the thing," said Charlie as he examined the trinket. "Where did you find it?"

"You remember the night we brought Ben and Cooper home?" Shintaro dragged the chain over to the side of his tub.

Charlie cocked his head to one side, "Yes…" he replied.

"Well, it's what I went back for," said Shintaro. "I think you pulled it off one of the bad people's necks when you were fighting with them. I was lying next to the truck, trying to get some air back into my lungs, and I saw this shiny thing being kicked around under everyone's feet." He laboriously tossed the dirty necklace into the tub, then jumped in after it.

"So, you went back for it when the action quieted down a

bit?" asked Charlie incredulously.

"You know how I am about those things. Besides, no one else seemed interested. So, I rescued it and hid it in the woods. The next evening, I retrieved it and stashed it here in the pen. If I dunk it in water, it gets all pretty again." He swished the necklace carefully through the water in his pond. Mud and dirt began to slowly wash off the prize. The lovely trinket was, once again, shiny and gold. Shintaro handed the sparkling clean necklace to Charlie, who gently laid it on the ground.

"It is a really big dangly doohickey to be wearing around one's neck," observed the chicken.

"Yeah, I know," said the proud duck as he took back the prized possession. He admired it for another minute, then dragged it back to its hiding place.

Chapter 17

The Interlopers

It was about this time that the lady in the high heels came back. But now she was very friendly and chatting with people in the town. She introduced herself as Louise Mitchell and mentioned that she was staying with her sister, Blanche, who had recently rented a small house at the edge of town.

Blanche kept to herself, so no one knew her, but Louise was constantly striking up conversations with people. She was particularly curious about the rescue of the kidnapped little boy earlier in the year. It seemed that she couldn't get enough of hearing the town folks' differing versions of the adventure. Each story was more harrowing than the next. She heard from everyone but the members of the Langdon family. They wouldn't talk about it. Granted, Louise could only ask them when she was at the store acting like she needed something. But when she brought it up, whoever was minding the store either ignored her or changed the subject.

One day she started asking if anyone had seen a necklace she had misplaced. She told folks that the heirloom had been missing for a few days. She was afraid it might have fallen off in the street or maybe in her sister's garden while she was planting flowers. No one had seen it. The prospect of finding the missing necklace was looking very bleak until the day she posed the question to Mrs. Downs.

"You might want to check with Molly Langdon," she suggested. "Her goofy duck likes to 'borrow' things, especially if they're shiny. Maybe he found it and tucked it away somewhere."

Louise trotted right over to the Langdon's store on her impossibly

spiked heels, but Molly assured her
that the duck had not left their
property for several weeks. The
woman was persistent. So, Lucy,
after Molly's urging, looked
through Shintaro's favorite hiding
spots and found nothing. Louise
scowled and demanded she be
allowed to look around the duck's
pen herself, but Molly said no.
Then she took the huffy visitor
firmly by the elbow and escorted
her off their property.

Two nights later, Charlie was
happily asleep in his Charlie Brown
tree, and Shintaro was tucked into a
nest of hay with his head under his
wing. Suddenly the quiet night was
disrupted by the crisp snap of a
twig breaking and the crunching of

pebbles on the gravel path. Charlie stood, but Shintaro stayed in his position, apparently trying to fool the perpetrator into thinking he was asleep. In truth, he was scared silly.

The footsteps reached the pen, and a light flashed into Shintaro's house. That was too much! Shintaro charged out of the hutch, quacking, hissing, and flapping his wings. Charlie flew down from his perch crowing, clucking, and trying to flap menacingly (this is very tricky indeed when one has only one wing that fully flaps). Lights came on in the house.

A person dressed all in black turned off the flashlight and took off over the gate, escaping through the bushes. Molly, Elliot, and Lucy came running out of the house, each armed with heavy objects: a baseball bat, a cast-iron skillet, and a bowling trophy. They stuck together as they looked around their yard. Nothing seemed to be amiss, so Lucy ran to check on the birds. Molly gave the all-clear, and they went back to bed.

"I'll call Sheriff Dean in the morning to let him know. It was probably just some kids being goofy," said Molly reassuringly.

Charlie and Shintaro settled back into their cozy pen, but Charlie couldn't sleep. Finally, he turned to Shintaro. "Where did you say you found that thing?" he asked.

Shintaro stared back at his friend. "By the truck the night we helped Ben escape. Why?"

"Methinks," said the very smart chicken, "that you have something very valuable there."

"Maybe," replied the duck, "but it's mine now. And I am not giving it back."

Charlie settled his body back down over his feet, fluffing his feathers warmly around himself. "Shintaro, my friend, I believe that was one of the kidnappers, and I believe that what you have will bring them out in the open. So, my fellow rescuer, we need to come up with a plan in which we trap some bad guys."

The two sat looking at the moon for a bit, contemplating their options. After that bit, a very short bit, as ducks have a very tiny attention span, Shintaro fell asleep. Charlie stayed awake a while, devising a plan.

The next morning, Sheriff Dean came by the Langdon home. Molly took him out to the birds' pen. The ground was dry, so there were no footprints. As the sheriff examined the bushes, he found a black button on the ground and some scraps of material hanging on a bush. "Well Molly, it looks like someone was here recently. That duck of yours would have found this button and tucked it away if it had been dropped more than a few hours ago."

Molly looked closely at the object the sheriff handed her. "That button looks like the kind on the work shirts that we sell at the store."

"But they're common, aren't they?" remarked the sheriff.

"We are the only ones who sell them in this area," said Molly.

The sheriff thought about this, then said, "See if you have any records of whom you sold this type of shirt to in the past couple of months."

"OK," said Molly, "but it will have to wait until tomorrow. Ben, Tom, and Cooper are coming in today."

"Just let me know what you find out," answered the sheriff as he got into his SUV and drove away.

Chapter 18

Friends

The Langdon home was all abuzz. Last-minute messes were picked up, bathrooms were cleaned, and cookies were made. The house sparkled, and the wonderful aroma of homemade baking wafted through every room, making the little home feel even more warm and welcoming than usual. Lucy had been glancing through the front window every chance she got in anticipation of Ben's arrival. When Lucy heard a car on the driveway, she was the first one out the door, bounding down the path. The car had barely stopped when the door flew open, and Cooper tumbled out. He burst through the gate and barged into Lucy. She fell to her knees as the joyous dog covered her face in big sloppy kisses. She giggled and hugged and kissed the big dog back. Tom came to her rescue, offering a strong hand to pull Lucy to her feet, and into a big bear hug.

When she finally saw Ben, they both smiled shyly at each other and waved hello. Then Lucy picked up one of the bags, and the two walked to the house together. Tom followed with the last suitcase. By the time he got to the front door, the kids were in the house, and Molly was waiting for him on the porch. He put the bag down and gave her a heartfelt hug. They followed their children into the home.

Elliot took the bags to the room that Ben and Tom would be sharing. Lucy took Ben out to see Charlie and Shintaro. Cooper rushed to greet the birds, and they flapped about in excitement. Lucy had warned them that Cooper was coming back, but they had forgotten how big and bouncy he was. Charlie jumped upon his

friend's back and Shintaro fell in
beside the two as they wandered to
the front porch and cuddled down
on the cushions that Lucy arranged
for them. The three comrades sat in
companionable silence while Ben
and Lucy talked, all of them feeling
safe and comfortable in each
other's company.

Chapter 19

The Trap

As the afternoon wore on, Charlie and Shintaro filled Cooper in on the strange happenings of the night before.

"Humph! I wonder what the intruder could have been looking for," Cooper mused.

Shintaro's eyes took on a

mischievous gleam. "I think they were after my treasure." He retold his adventure of retrieving the shiny necklace.

"Have you thought about using it to trap them? What if you let them know you have it and then catch them trying to retrieve it?" suggested Cooper.

"How do we do that?" asked both birds at the same time.

"We're not even sure who they are," added Charlie.

"If they tried to break in, they're probably watching this place, right?" said the dog.

"Yeah, so?" said the duck.

"Well, Shintaro, you need to

flaunt that shiny trinket."

"How do I do that without Lucy seeing it?"

Cooper wiggled his eyebrows and said, "You know who belongs here and who doesn't right? So, show it off to the people whom you don't know too well or don't trust. See what happens."

Charlie thought this was a great idea. Shintaro was skeptical, but he waddled off to dig up his treasure. Once he had recovered the necklace and cleaned it up again, the two birds made their way up to the front of the store. The feathered spies tucked themselves deep inside a lilac bush and waited for someone to come down the sidewalk.

Shintaro held the necklace close to his body. If he saw someone he didn't know, he would waddle out and pretend to be picking at the necklace on the ground. It was the end of summer and most of the tourists had left already. Charlie and Shintaro knew everyone who came by, so the afternoon wore on very slowly.

While the birds waited for their prey in front of the store, Cooper was inside the store keeping a watchful eye on Ben. The children were helping Elliot stock shelves. Cooper curled up on a dog bed by the front window and dozed, waking occasionally to check on his boy. A few minutes before closing time, the old brass

cowbell that hung on the door
jingled, and three people entered.
Cooper watched their feet as they
walked through the store: two
women and a man. From Cooper's
vantage point on the floor, he
noticed that the man was wearing
black jeans and black boots. One of
the women had on blue jeans and
white tennis shoes, and the other
was in a dress and wearing high
heels. They didn't seem very
interesting, so Cooper yawned and
put his head down.

The woman in jeans went over
to talk to Elliot about getting some
supplies. The man and the high-
heeled woman began talking
quietly by the counter, unaware that
Lucy and Ben were sitting on the

floor on the other side, sorting some items for the display case. Suddenly, Cooper's ears perked up. What had the man just said? He sounded familiar. Before Cooper could get up to investigate, the woman in sensible shoes came back and they all left.

Fleas, I hope Shintaro sees them, thought Cooper. He carefully lumbered out the doggie door and was just in time to see Shintaro go into his act of 'find the necklace'.

As the strangers approached the shiny thing that hadn't been there a moment ago, Shintaro waddled out nonchalantly and started to peck at it, moving it just enough so that the locket flashed in the remaining sunlight. It took the humans a few seconds to figure out what Shintaro had, but as soon as they realized what it was, all three lunged at the little duck.

The giddy bird happily grabbed up the treasure and started running gleefully around in circles, in and out and around the three sets of legs, his wings flapping. The three hapless humans tried desperately to grab the speedy duck, but he was too fast for them. Shintaro stayed just out of reach. He was having the time of his life, but when a finger brushed his tail, he decided to make his escape. The excited duck ran away into the bushes and back toward the house, the treasure flying behind him.

The three strangers untangled

themselves and looked around in confusion. They saw a group of teenagers coming toward them from one direction, and in the other, a big black dog was guarding Shintaro's escape route. The dog's teeth were bared, and the hair on his back was standing up. He growled. The man and two women turned and hustled off in the other direction.

Cooper hurried back into the store. Elliot was kneeling next to Lucy and Ben. Ben had his arms around his knees. He was rocking back and forth, shaking.

"It was him, Lucy. It was the guy who took me, " gasped the little boy.

Lucy gently put her arm around her friend and asked, "How do you know?"

"In the truck as we were driving, he got irritated with the person in the front seat and he said, 'Jeez Louise stop clicking your nails.' he said it several times. That guy who was just here said it too. Just like the man in the truck!"

"We've got to tell Mom and Tom," said Elliot. They quickly locked up the store, and with his arms protectively around the two younger children, Elliot ran Lucy and Ben up to the house. Molly and Tom were making spaghetti as the kids stumbled into the kitchen. Tom took one look at the expression on Ben's face, dropped the sauce spoon, put his arms around his son, and led him to the recliner in the living room.

Ben kept saying in a shaky voice, "It was him, Dad, it was him. He's here."

Molly handed the frightened boy a glass of water and joined her two children on the couch. "As calmly as you can," Molly said, "please tell us what happened."

All three kids started to speak at once.

"One at a time guys," directed Tom. "Ben, you go first. Whom did you see?"

In between gasps for air and small sobs, Ben described what he had heard in the store. Halfway through the story, Molly called Sheriff Dean. He said he would be right out.

Meanwhile, Cooper reconnoitered with the two birds, telling them what he had heard. He too had recognized the kidnapper's voice. They figured that the man would probably be back later that night. He obviously wanted the necklace.

It was starting to get dark, and the wind was picking up. While they were talking, a piece of fruit flew over the wall into the coop. Shintaro went to check out the morsel, but Cooper stopped him. He sniffed it. It looked like an ordinary slice of cantaloupe, but it smelled funny.

"A friend of mine ate something that was thrown over his wall once and fell asleep," warned Cooper. "His master's house was robbed that night. This could be the same kind of trick, don't you think?"

"It could be," countered the chicken, "Let's assume that that thing is supposed to knock us out for a while. We can pretend to be asleep, just like they want. It's the perfect trap."

Cooper buried the fruit, and Shintaro laid his treasure carelessly in the hutch, covering it lightly with dirt so it would be easy to find.

Chapter 20

The Sting

That night, a thunderstorm blew in. The trees rattled, and cold rain pelted the birds' enclosure. The wind was blowing so hard it looked as if the rain was coming down sideways. Shintaro and Charlie hid; Charlie up in the bushes and Shintaro behind his hutch. They had piled up feathers and hay to look like two sleeping birds. Cooper was lying under the bushes near the back door of the house. His black fur blended into the shadows. The three secret agents, for that's what they felt like, lay in wait for what seemed like hours.

Shintaro, not one to stay still for very long at the best of times, was beginning to fidget and fuss. Charlie stirred slightly to cluck a short warning to his friend to be quiet. A moment later, they heard crunching pebbles. Whoever was walking up the path was very near the bird pen, but it was still hard to hear anything over the noise of the driving rain.

The gate rattled open. The intruder entered the pen and began looking in every nook and cranny. Finally, the thief inspected the inside of Shintaro's house and found the necklace right where the clever bird had planned. Grabbing it, the perpetrator hurried through the gate and down the path shoving the trinket into his jean's pocket as he went. Suddenly he felt the force of large paws pushing on his chest knocking him backward into the mud. The crook found himself pinned to the ground by Cooper. The dog's face loomed inches away from the helpless human, lips curled back, a menacing growl warning the man not to move.

Charlie was instantly by the dog's side flapping his wings and scratching at the ski mask, squawking wildly. Shintaro was quick to join in, clinging furiously to the gloved hands to keep anything from hurting Charlie.

The thief bellowed hideously for help. Lights came on all over the house, but this time, not only did the family rush through the rain to the coop with their makeshift weapons, but Sheriff Dean came running from the front gate, gun drawn, yelling for the man to stay down.

The man yelled back, "I couldn't get up if I wanted to!" Tom ordered Cooper to get off; Elliot removed Charlie from the prisoner's face; and Lucy carefully picked the frantic duck up off the ground where he was still pecking at the fallen villain's arm.

Chapter 21

Conquering Heroes

"Whew, that was tense," said Shintaro as the three animals sat calmly together on the front porch, eating the treats that Molly had provided. It had been several hours since they had apprehended the villain and they were finally settling down.

"I'm sure glad the sheriff

came by when he did," said Cooper. "That guy was a lot stronger than he looked." The three friends curled up in their favorite sleeping positions. Two snuggled their heads under their wings, and one tucked his nose under his tail. Then all three drifted off into much-needed slumber.

Molly, Tom, and Sheriff Dean came out to the front porch. The storm had calmed to a light rain, so they didn't have to shout to be heard over the thunder.

"Your hunch paid off, Sheriff," said Tom. "The kidnappers did come back for that necklace. What was so important about it?"

"We don't know all the details yet," said the lawman, "but there is some sort of key inside the locket that is attached to the necklace. Looks like maybe a safe deposit box key. We'll know more tomorrow. Deputy Swinney and a couple of officers found our kidnapper's cohorts waiting in a car down the road a piece." The sheriff started toward the porch steps, stopped, and turned to look at the three sleeping animals. "You have some very brave friends there, Molly. They made my job a lot easier. Take good care of them."

The tired parents smiled down at the animals as the sheriff drove away. Tom put his arms around Molly's shoulder.

"Such an odd assortment of friends they are," said Molly. "We owe them so much. I wonder if they will ever know how grateful we are and how much we love them."

"They know," Tom said with a smile.

Chapter 22

Sheriff Dean Fills It All In

Several days passed before the whole story came out. Everyone was waiting on the front porch when Sheriff Dean arrived. The law officer picked up one of Molly's freshly baked cookies and began his story. "Our three kidnappers were Mike Bridges, his wife Louise Bridges, and her mother Blanche

Mitchell. They got the idea of kidnapping a rich kid after watching a TV show. Mike was a gardener in Tom's neighborhood, so he had the perfect opportunity to watch your household and figure out your schedule. When he realized you were coming out here for a hiking trip earlier this summer, they set their trap.

When they kidnapped Ben, they demanded a ransom in diamonds. You were anxious to keep your son from harm and delivered the ransom, which Blanche put in a safe deposit box. She kept the key in a locket. Everything was going smoothly. They were going to move Ben to the drop-off location and get out of town, but then these crazy animals attacked, and Ben escaped. Somewhere in all that mayhem the duck got the necklace with the key to the diamonds and brought it back to the house."

Sheriff Dean took a swig of the ice-cold lemonade and looked at the now peaceful duck basking in the sun.

"How did the bad guys know it was here?' asked Lucy.

"They didn't," the sheriff replied, "they just knew it wasn't at the cabin where they'd been attacked, so they assumed someone picked it up. That's why they were asking questions all over town. We found Blanche's name in your store's system because she used her credit card to buy a shirt around that time. When Louise heard that Shintaro had a history of collecting shiny treasures, Mike tried to break in to search the duck's house."

"At this point, they probably knew that their animal attackers had been Shin and Charlie, right?" said Elliot.

"Yup," said the sheriff, "and when they saw Ben was back in town, they knew they had to retrieve the necklace and leave town quickly."

"When I heard that man say, 'Jeez Louise', I thought he was using the expression my mom always uses when she is frustrated about something," said Ben, "but he was actually saying Jeez, Louise, as in his wife's name Louise. I think that's kind of funny." They all chuckled together on the porch, drinking their lemonade, and eating their cookies.

"Well, we have all the evidence we need to make sure they never bother you again, son," the sheriff assured Ben.

Lucy hopped off the porch and hugged Shintaro. He snuggled against her neck, his curved beak making it look like he was smiling. "I guess it's a good thing you never listened when we told you to stay out of trouble," said Lucy.

Epilogue

A few days before Ben, Tom, and Cooper had to go home, they all went on a camping trip in the mountains, even Shintaro and Charlie. It was a great time, and they agreed they would have to make it an annual tradition.

After breakfast the morning they returned from camping, Lucy and Ben sat on the edge of the porch while the adults made one more check of the house for forgotten items. The children looked out at the peaceful front yard with the giant oak tree.

Finally, Ben said, "I am going to miss you, Lucy."

"Me too. Will you email?"

"You bet. Every day."

Tom came out on the porch with suitcases in hand. He called for Cooper. The big dog came trotting around the corner of the house, a bird on each side. Elliot brought out another bag, and Molly appeared with freshly baked cookies "for the road."

Tom personally thanked each

of them, offering hugs to Lucy, Elliott, and Molly, and even thanked the birds. Ben also shook Elliot's hand and hugged Molly with many thanks. Ben hugged Lucy last, then ran to the car, calling for Cooper. Cooper looked at his two bird friends. The big dog bent down on his front legs as if bowing to them and barked one woof before jumping into the car. Finally, Tom hugged Molly and kissed her softly on the cheek. "Thank you for everything. Ben and I owe your family so much."

She smiled and said, "We'll always be here for you, Ben, and Cooper." The Langdons watched the Lawrences drive away, then walked into the now-silent house.

Charlie and Shintaro began the long walk to their pen. They stopped short when they heard a familiar, but dreaded sound.

"Well, that was touching," said Bruno snidely from atop the porch roof where he sat cleaning his tail. The cat, balanced on his rump, one hind leg stuck straight up in the air, was all twisted up, as only cats can do to reach the right spot. With a sneer in his voice, he said, "I'm going to have to curl up in a box of tissues as I am just awash with tears."

With ruffled feathers, Charlie and Shintaro looked up at the nasty foe, both ready to snap some equally snide remark back. Then just as quickly, they stopped, and smiles emerged on their beaks.

"You will never again ruffle our feathers, Bruno," said Charlie.

"True," said Shintaro, "because we know what you really are."

"Oh yeah? What's that?" sneered the cat.

Together the birds looked up at the feckless feline and said, "Our friend." Bruno was speechless as he watched the two feathered heroes meander down the path to their cozy coop.